Mrs.
Emerick

This book is for Michael Dante

Atheneum Books for Young Readers
An imprint of Simon & Schuster Children's Publishing Division
1230 Avenue of the Americas
New York, New York 10020

Book design by Michael Nelson

The text of this book is set in Avenir.
The illustrations are rendered in gouache on watercolor paper.

Printed in Hong Kong
10 9 8 7 6 5 4 3 2

Library of Congress Cataloging-in-Publication Data
Yaccarino, Dan.
Deep in the jungle / written and illustrated by Dan Yaccarino.—1st ed.
p.   cm.
"An Anne Schwartz book."
Summary: After being tricked into joining the circus,
an arrogant lion escapes and returns to the jungle where he lives
peacefully with the animals he used to terrorize.
ISBN 0-689-82235-9
[1. Lions—Fiction. 2. Jungle animals—Fiction. 3. Circus—Fiction.] I. Title.
PZ7.Y125De 1999   [E]—dc21   98-24088

DEEP IN THE JUNGLE

written and illustrated by

Dan Yaccarino

An ANNE SCHWARTZ BOOK

ATHENEUM BOOKS for YOUNG READERS

Deep in the jungle, the mighty lion roared for the monkeys to fan him faster. It was a very hot day indeed. He reminded them that he was their ruler. "I'm afraid I must eat you," he explained, "if you don't obey me." The monkeys fanned faster.

The lion was king of this jungle and he made sure *everyone* knew it. The leopards brought him food, the gorillas brushed his mane, and the elephants gave him shade. The animals couldn't stand him one bit.

One day, while the animals were picking bananas for the almighty king, a man was seen roaming through the jungle. The monkeys ran and told the lion.

"Oh, very well." The lion yawned. "I'll take a look. I was bored anyway."

So the lion slunk through the bushes and vines until he spotted the man.

"Rrrrroar!" he hollered, and leaped on top of the surprised man, who, incidentally, looked like he would make a lovely dinner. "I am the king of this jungle! Now prepare to be eaten!

"Rrrrroar!" he added.

"Hmm, that's quite good," said the man. "Could you do that again, this time with a little more feeling?"

The lion was confused, but pleased to meet someone who knew a good roar when he heard one.

"RRRRROAR!" The lion almost busted a gut.

"Beautiful!" said the man. "You know, you're wasting your time here, lion. Come with me and I'll make you a big star!"

The lion, who never thought he was much appreciated anyway, agreed.

The animals were more than happy to be rid of him.

The lion and his new friend walked through the jungle to a small railroad station, where the man bought a ticket for himself and a baggage claim for the lion. "I'm afraid you must ride in the luggage car," the man explained. "But don't worry, it's a short trip." The lion was so excited about becoming famous, he didn't particularly care.

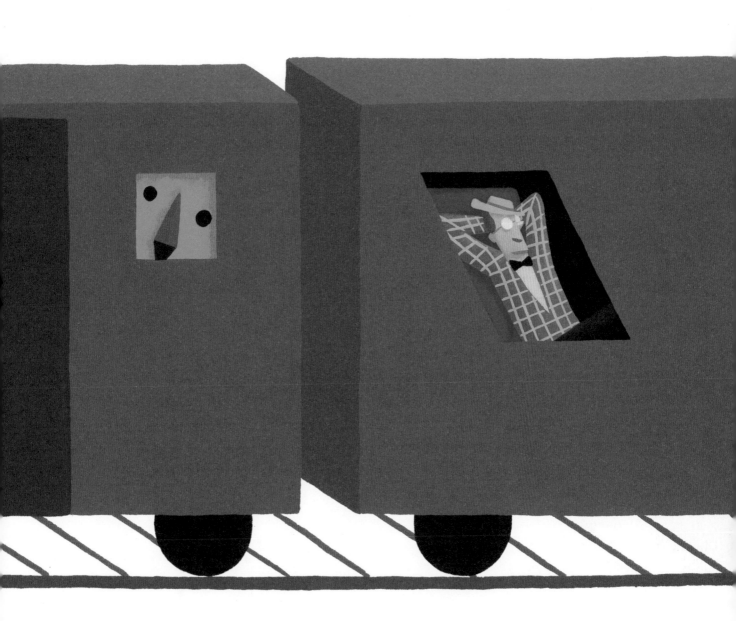

The train rattled on and on. As he looked through
the small window, the lion recognized less and less.
He was far from his jungle.

At last, the train pulled into a station. "I'm afraid I must put this leash on you, lion. It's the law, you know," said the man, meeting the lion at the door.

So the king of the jungle lowered his head, the man put the leash around his neck, and off they went.

It was very exciting for the lion to be inside a colorful circus tent. The man and the lion walked up to a cage with thick iron bars. "And now I'm afraid I must put you in here," the man said. "It'll be a good career move for you. Trust me."

So the king of the jungle lowered his head once more, walked into the cage, and the gate slammed shut. *Hmm*, he thought, *I wonder if this is how all the big stars start out?*

Soon the lion fell asleep. He had wonderful dreams
of roaring his amazing roar before capacity crowds.

The people cheered wildly, threw roses, and demanded an encore.

Crack! The sound of a whip woke him from his blissful slumber. It was the man, all in costume. "Wake up, ol' boy," he demanded. "It's showtime."

"What's the meaning of the whip?" asked the lion. "Certainly there's no need for *that*."

"I'm afraid I must use this whip," the man explained, "but don't think twice about it. Showbiz, you know."

He cracked it a few more times, just for effect, of course, and led the lion out to the center ring. It was so loud, crowded, and confusing that the lion became nervous. He was about to let out a mighty crowd-pleasing roar when—

Crack! Crack! The man snapped the whip . . . a little too close to the lion's nose. The lion backed up as the man waved a chair at him. *Crack!* "Up onto the platform!" demanded the man. *Crack! Crack!*

So the lion climbed up. Everyone cheered wildly, but it was not for the lion, it was for the *man.*

Here I am doing all the work, thought the lion, *and he's getting all the applause!*

Night after night this went on. And night after night the lion grew more and more tired of obeying while he waited for his big break. Finally, he approached the man.

"Look, when will I get to perform my solo?" he asked. "First, I'll let out my mighty roar, then . . ."

"Now, just hold on there, ol' boy," said the man. "I'm afraid you must always obey me. Showbiz, you know." He cracked the whip.

The lion thought for a moment. "Well then, I'm afraid I must eat you up. Jungle law, you know," he replied. And he swallowed the man, one gulp, right down.

The lion made up his mind. He had a bellyful of show business, and he was going home.

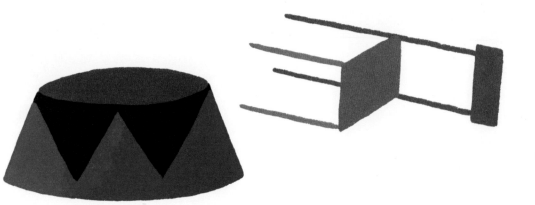

Just for good measure, he roared the loudest, earth-shakingest, tent-rattlingest roar ever.

Then he took a bow and walked right out of the circus tent.

The lion walked and walked until he came to the railroad station where he'd arrived with the man, who, by the way, was now giving him indigestion.

The lion followed the train tracks and, as he did, thought about all the animals in the jungle. He could hardly wait to get home.

At last the lion reached the trees and vines. He was about to let out a roar of joy when he came upon a startling sight. Before him stood a man locking all the animals into cages with thick iron bars.

"Oh, look who's here," said the giraffe miserably. "It's that lousy lion."

"So sorry we can't tend to your every whim at the moment, oh mighty king," said the gorilla.

The lion was hurt by the animals' harsh words. He wanted to leave, but suddenly he knew what he had to do.

The lion turned to the man.

"Sir, this is a sorry collection of animals you have, to be sure," he said. "What you need is a mighty lion. *King of the Jungle.*"

"Oh, boy," said an elephant, "there he goes again."

"Can you perform any tricks?" asked the man.

"Can *I* perform tricks? My dear fellow, my specialty is the famous 'man's-head-in-the-lion's-mouth trick,'" he proudly replied.

Thrilled, the man asked the lion to show him.

"I'd be delighted," said the lion.

So the man stuck his head right in the lion's mouth, and, well, you can figure out the rest.

Then the lion set all the animals free. "I'm afraid I owe you an apology," he said to every one of them. "Silly pride and all."
And from that day on, the lion never roared at anyone ever again.

Except, of course, when he was giving a concert. The animals
cheered wildly, threw roses, and demanded encores. The lion
was only too happy to oblige. Showbiz, you know.